Emma Thomson's

# felicity Wishes®

# Sensational Secrets

and other stories

Hodder
Children's
Books

A division of Hodder Headline Limited

# How to make your felicity Wishes

## WISH

With this book comes an extra special wish for you and your best friend.

Hold the book together at each end and both close your eyes.

Wriggle your noses and think of a number under ten.

Open your eyes, whisper the numbers you thought of to each other.

Add these numbers together. This is your

### Magic Number

*you*

*best friend*

Place your little finger on the stars, and say your magic number out loud together. Now make your wish quietly to yourselves. And maybe, one day, your wish might just come true.    Love

*felicity*

x

For Bridget Alice Rani Calthrop
with sparkling wishes
E. V. T

Emma Thomson's
felicity Wishes®

FELICITY WISHES
Felicity Wishes © 2000 Emma Thomson
Licensed by White Lion Publishing

Text and Illustrations © 2005 Emma Thomson

First published in Great Britain in 2005 by Hodder Children's Books

The right of Emma Thomson to be identified as the author and illustrator of this work has
been asserted by her in accordance with the Copyright, Designs and Patents Act 1988.

2 4 6 8 10 9 7 5 3

A Catalogue record for this book is available from the British Library

ISBN 0 340 90242 6

Printed and bound in China by Imago

The paper and board used in this paperback by Hodder Children's Books are natural recyclable
products made from wood grown in sustainable forests. The manufacturing processes
conform to the environmental regulations of the country of origin.

Hodder Children's Books
A division of Hodder Headline Ltd, 338 Euston Road, London NW1 3BH

# CONTENTS

# Sensational Secrets

"There's something very familiar about that fairy," whispered Felicity Wishes to her best friends in assembly.

"Yes," said Polly. "I know her from somewhere but I just can't put my wand on it."

"Maybe we've seen her in Sparkles?" suggested Daisy.

"Or maybe she's someone famous," said Holly, overdoing it. Holly was always the most dramatic fairy in the group.

Fairy Godmother was on stage,

introducing a very shy-looking fairy with beautiful curly auburn hair. The fairy friends stared intently at her.

"Fairies, this is Ella. She will be joining the School of Nine Wishes for a short time to sit her final exams. I hope that while she is with us you will all make her feel very welcome."

"Actually, I think she is someone famous," said Felicity, forgetting to whisper.

"FELICITY WISHES!" Miss Meandering's voice boomed across the hall. "You should know better than talking in assembly. See Fairy Godmother after school for detention."

It was the fourth time that week Felicity had been told off for talking when she shouldn't. Sometimes she got so swept up in conversation she forgot where she was.

* * *

After school Felicity waited outside

Fairy Godmother's office, playing idly with the ends of her wand.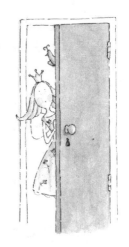

She noticed a crack in the door and peeped inside the office. Fairy Godmother was talking to the new fairy, Ella. Curiosity got the better of Felicity and she moved in closer so she could hear what they were discussing.

"I know these exams aren't strictly necessary but nevertheless I'm glad you've taken the decision to sit them. It is an honour that you've chosen the School of Nine Wishes, and remember, if you need anything, then please don't hesitate to come straight to me." With that Fairy Godmother opened the door.

"Oh, Felicity, I didn't know you were there," she said, suddenly flustered.

"Miss Meandering asked me to see you," said Felicity looking sheepish. "I was talking in assembly."

Expecting to be told off, Felicity was surprised when Fairy Godmother said "Oh never mind that. The important thing is to make Ella feel at home. Can you show her around the school and make sure she settles in OK?"

For Felicity this was hardly a punishment as she was naturally one of the friendliest fairies in the School of Nine Wishes. There wasn't anything Felicity enjoyed doing more than making friends.

\* \* \*

The following day Felicity and Ella flew through classrooms, games rooms and grounds until they had covered just about everything.

Felicity tried to chat to Ella about

her last school but although Ella
seemed friendly, it was obvious that
she didn't want to talk about herself
or her friends. Felicity was baffled –
who wouldn't want to talk about their
friends?

But Ella was very interested in
Felicity's friends, so Felicity soon
forgot about their odd conversation
and filled Ella in on all the gossip.
She could talk about her friends
forever.

"...and Holly is the most fashionable
fairy I know," Felicity continued after
at least thirty minutes. "She's going
to make the most beautiful Christmas
Fairy when she graduates."

Felicity landed with an
exhausted thud in the
dining hall. "I don't
know about you, but
after all this flying
I'm starving!"

"Goodness, yes," said Ella, speaking for the first time in ages!

The lunch-time bell rang and then suddenly the dining hall was full of hundreds of hungry fairies.

"Hi there," said Felicity as Holly, Polly and Daisy sat down to join them.

"This is Ella, you probably recognise her from assembly," said Felicity introducing her to everyone.

"Yes!" said Polly excitedly. "You do have a very familiar face," she said still trying to work out where she knew her from.

Slightly embarrassed, Ella hid her face behind her auburn curls. "You probably do recognise me – I'm very well known in some circles."

Holly, Polly, Daisy and Felicity stopped eating and looked at her in anticipation.

"I used to work in Fairy Mart on Saturdays. I think I can remember

you coming in to buy Fairy Girl," Ella
added.

"Fairy Mart!" said Holly,
disappointed. "I thought you were
someone famous!"

"And I thought I'd seen
your face in a magazine
recently," said Daisy
agreeing.

Ella blushed. "O-Oh no,"
she stuttered. "Only Fairy Mart!"

✳ ✳ ✳

At the end of a long day, Felicity and
her friends met up, as they often did,
by the school gate.

"Let's wait for Ella," suggested
Felicity, "to see if she wants to come
to Sparkles for a hot chocolate."

"I've just seen her flying down the
road," said Holly.

"Oh, that's a shame. I was looking
forward to getting to know her better,"
said Daisy disappointed.

"I'll try and catch up with her,"
said Felicity flapping her wings. "I'm
sure she'd love to come along too."
And with that Felicity dashed off in
Ella's direction.

Felicity flew as fast as she could
but when she got to the end of the
road, Ella was almost out of sight.
Felicity quickly rounded the corner,
just in time to see Ella fluttering

into a stretched black limousine!

None of it made any sense, Felicity thought. What was Ella doing in a limousine? Why did Fairy Godmother say she didn't need to sit her exams? And who was she really?

"Ella has a secret," Felicity whispered to herself, "and I'm going to find out what it is!"

Flying high so she wasn't noticed, Felicity followed the limousine as it wound its way over hills and down long lanes, until at last it came to a stop outside a large country mansion.

Hovering silently behind a cloud, Felicity watched as Ella got out of the limousine and entered the big house. Suddenly Felicity felt silly. She shouldn't be spying on her new friend when she could just ask her tomorrow. She turned to leave but then the front door opened again.

Out walked a fairy with the longest, straightest blonde hair Felicity had ever seen.

Daring to fly closer to get a better look, Felicity lost her balance and before she knew what was happening she was tumbling through the sky at an uncontrollable speed.

She landed with a thump right at the feet of the fairy.

When Felicity looked up she thought she was dreaming.

"Wow!" said Felicity. It was Jolie, the most successful international pop idol in the whole of fairy world.

"Let me give you a hand," said Jolie, picking Felicity up off the floor.

Felicity dusted herself down. "Wow!" she said again, completely starstruck. Jolie was Felicity's pop idol and she couldn't believe she was standing here in front of her.

"Can I help you?" said Jolie, amused.

"Umm…" said Felicity, stuck for words.

"I was here to ask if Ella wanted to come to Sparkles for a hot chocolate," said Felicity.

Jolie looked confused for a moment.

"Oh, Ella!" she said, laughing and looking a little relieved. "Yes, Ella! She's, um, staying with me at the moment while she takes her exams."

"Would you both like to come to Sparkles?" asked Felicity.

"That might be a bit difficult," said Jolie mysteriously. "Ella and I can't be seen together. It's a secret that I'm here at all."

"I understand," said Felicity nodding solemnly. "Well, please could you let her know that I called and say I'll see her at school tomorrow."

"Of course," said Jolie. She waved as Felicity flew off, wings wobbling with excitement.

* * *

"What took you so long?" said Polly

when Felicity arrived at Sparkles. "Did you catch up with Ella?"

Felicity slumped down in a chair. She was exhausted from all the flying.

"You wouldn't believe it even if I told you, which I can't because it's a secret!" said Felicity mysteriously. She knew that keeping this secret from her friends would be very difficult but she had to do it for Jolie's sake.

"Well, we have a secret too!" said Holly, Polly and Daisy together, quickly hiding their copy of Fairy Girl, "and we can't tell you!"

Felicity was dying to know what her friends' secret was but she knew she couldn't tell them her secret so she quickly put it to the back of her mind.

* * *

The next day at school Felicity didn't have to find Ella. It was Ella that found her first.

"You look terrible," said Felicity,

noticing the bags under Ella's eyes.

"I didn't sleep last night," whispered Ella. "Where can we go to talk, secretly?"

Felicity led Ella to a secret place where she was sure no one would find them. It was a long forgotten greenhouse at the back of the school playing field, overgrown with long leafy vines and creeping brambles.

"Watch your head," said Felicity as she parted the dense greenery.

"Right," she said once they were both safe inside. "No one knows we're here and no one can hear us. What did you want to tell me?"

"Oh Felicity!" said Ella, suddenly bursting into tears, "The press have found out that Jolie is staying somewhere

in the countryside near Bloomfield!"

"I can't believe you know her!" said Felicity. "When I followed you to ask if you'd like to go to Sparkles I never in a million fairy years imagined that I'd end up meeting Jolie! She's so famous!"

"You didn't tell anyone, did you?" said Ella quickly.

"No, no! Of course not," said Felicity slightly offended. She always prided herself on keeping secrets safe.

Ella looked relieved. "Well," she said, "it's an even bigger secret now. If the press find out that Jolie is here then she'll have to leave and I won't be able to sit my exams."

"Why can't you stay if she goes?" asked Felicity.

Ella looked awkward for a moment.

"We go everywhere together. Jolie doesn't have very many friends because she finds it so hard to trust people. It's very difficult for her to lead a normal life. Nothing is private and everything she does ends up in the press."

Big tears welled up in Ella's eyes.

"Don't worry, I'll do all I can to help you keep your secret safe," said Felicity giving Ella the biggest friendship hug.

"Thank you," said Ella making her way out of the greenhouse. She bent down and as she dipped to squeeze through the undergrowth, a bramble tugged at her hair.

Just for a second, the bramble lifted up Ella's large auburn curls to reveal a head of beautiful long blonde hair! Felicity gasped. Ella's hair was a wig, and underneath she was Jolie!

\* \* \*

Jolie had no idea that Felicity knew her identity, but for the next few weeks at school, Felicity did everything she could to keep her friend's secret safe.

When she heard fairies wondering where they knew her from, Felicity managed to persuade them that they recognised her from Fairy Mart.

When reporters asked questions in Sparkles, Felicity distracted them with fake sightings of Jolie on Bird Island.

Even when Ella's wig sometimes slipped Felicity always managed to tug it back into place without anyone noticing, not even Ella!

✳ ✳ ✳

The day that Ella finally sat her exams, Felicity was delighted that they'd managed to keep her secret safe, but also a little sad that her new friend would be leaving.

"I'll miss you," said Ella to Felicity when they finally had to say goodbye.

"You've been a true friend to me and, more importantly, a trustworthy friend."

"And to Jolie!" said Felicity, knowingly.

"You know!" said Jolie, stunned.

"For ages!" said Felicity, giggling. "But I have kept your secret safe."

"Well, now I've done my exams it doesn't have to be a secret any more," said Jolie, as she pulled off her wig and let her long blonde hair tumble out.

Fairies all around suddenly stopped and stared at Jolie. Felicity couldn't help laughing at their shocked faces when they realised that Ella was none other than the famous, international popstar.

* * *

"I've got something amazing to tell you," said Felicity when she joined Holly, Polly and Daisy after school.

"Ella was really the famous pop star Jolie in disguise!"

"Oh, you knew?" said Holly surprised. "We didn't tell you because we'd thought you'd tell everyone!"

"What do you mean?" said Felicity confused. "You knew?"

"We found out the day you asked Ella to join us in Sparkles," said Daisy. "There was a whole article in Fairy Girl about how Jolie wanted to take her exams and had moved somewhere near Bloomfield!"

"When we saw the picture all you had to do was draw on some curly hair and we recognised her immediately," explained Polly.

"But you never said anything," said Felicity shocked.

"And neither did you!" chorused the others.

"Well I guess that's what makes a secret secret!" said Felicity giggling.

Trust good friends
to keep secrets
you'd sometimes
rather not share

# Chocolate Cover-up

"OK, it's a deal!" said Felicity Wishes confidently to each of her friends, shaking their hands one by one.

Holly, Polly, and Daisy were convinced Felicity would find it impossible to give up chocolate but Felicity was determined to prove them wrong! All the fairies had decided to give up chocolate for a whole month.

"You know that no chocolate means no hot chocolate as well," said Polly, making the rules clear.

"And no chocolate milkshake either," said Daisy.

"Not even chocolate bubble gum," said Holly,

"OK, OK!" said Felicity determinedly. "I'm sure I can do it," she said, sounding more confident than she felt.

"Not the tiniest bit of chocolate is to pass our lips for one whole month or else we have to tell our deepest, darkest secrets!" said Polly.

Felicity winced. She had lots of secrets but wasn't sure she wanted to share them with everyone.

\* \* \*

Giving up chocolate was tougher than Felicity had expected. By the third day, she wasn't just dreaming of chocolate at night, she was also thinking about it for most of the day as well!

"What is this?" said Miss Sparkle,

the chemistry teacher, when she came to inspect Felicity's work.

"It's grade two sparkledust, Miss," said Felicity, looking down at the twinkling grains in her dish.

"No it's not, Felicity. It's superior grade chocolate powder," said Miss Sparkle, dipping her finger in and licking it.

"When you're making something magical you have to concentrate.

Whatever you're thinking about is bound to have an effect on what you produce. Please try again and this time Felicity really think about what you are doing."

Felicity hung her head low and started the experiment all over again.

Holly, Polly and Daisy looked at each other across the classroom. They were now more certain than ever that Felicity was going to break their pact.

\* \* \*

None of the other lessons were proving any easier either.

Felicity's energy levels in games class were much lower without her lunch-time chocolate sparkle bar to give her a boost. In maths they had to count chocolate buttons and the temptation was nearly too much for Felicity. And the chocolate chip cookies she made in cooking class just didn't taste the same without any chocolate chips!

At the end of the first week, Felicity was going crazy without chocolate. Everywhere she looked she saw chocolate – hills turned into chocolate cakes, the sun into a chocolate biscuit and streams into hot chocolate!

"Who would know?" she said to herself as she fluttered into her kitchen and rummaged around in her 'sweetie drawer'. It was crammed full with every kind of chocolate treat available. Felicity drooled at the dark Belgian chocolate she had been saving for a special occasion. She sniffed the jar of super-strength cocoa powder as she imagined curling up on the sofa with a mug of hot chocolate. And, even though they were very small, the chocolate sprinkles would be more than enough to curb her chocolate craving.

Enough was enough! Felicity quickly closed the curtains, frantically checked outside the front door, looked over both shoulders and then slowly, ever so slowly, savouring the moment, she unwrapped a chocolate bar and popped a square of chocolate into her mouth. It was delicious.

Felicity hadn't meant to cheat but she knew her limits. By her calculations one tiny square of chocolate a day would be just enough to keep her going until the end of the month, and that wasn't really so bad, was it? She counted out just enough squares of chocolate for one a day until the end of the month and put them in her most secret place – her Secrets Box.

\* \* \*

"Felicity seems to be coping very well without chocolate this week," said Polly to Holly and Daisy.

Polly wanted to be a tooth fairy one day and didn't really have a sweet tooth so was finding it all rather easy. Holly and Daisy were struggling but certainly wouldn't admit it in front of Polly.

"Yes," agreed Daisy. "Maybe she's over the worst of the cravings."

"Unless she's cheating!" said Holly suspiciously. "I think we should pay her a surprise visit to check."

"We can't do that!" said Polly astounded. "I'm sure Felicity wouldn't cheat. We always do everything together and this is no exception."

"But we could just call round to say 'hello'," said Daisy, who had to agree that Felicity didn't have lots of willpower at the best of times.

\* \* \*

Luckily for Felicity she had just swallowed her once-a-day chocolate treat when Holly, Polly and Daisy walked through her back door unannounced.

"Oh hello!" said Felicity, blushing with guilt. "What a nice surprise!"

"I hope you don't mind us popping in like this, but we were just passing," said Polly, noting that all the curtains were closed. "It's a bit dark in here."

"Um, yes," said Felicity, frantically putting her Secrets Box back in the drawer. "I was feeling a bit sleepy so thought I would go to bed." Felicity didn't like lying to her friends but also didn't want to disappoint them with the truth.

"But it's the middle of the afternoon," said Holly suspiciously.

"I think it's the lack of chocolate," said Felicity, secretly pleased with herself for thinking up such a good answer.

"Well, we had better leave you to your sleep then," suggested Polly. "We can make our own way out."

Reluctantly Felicity said goodbye to her friends and headed upstairs to bed. She would much rather be spending time with her friends than cooped up indoors on her own.

\* \* \*

"I don't think she is cheating," said Daisy as they gathered their things to leave.

"No, not if she's tired in the afternoon," said Polly, convinced by Felicity's story.

"There would be evidence if she had been sneaking chocolate," said

Holly, bending down to pick up her bag. "LIKE THIS!" she held up a small golden chocolate wrapper.

It didn't take them long to find the source. The half-open drawer bulged with the Secrets Box, clearly displaying Felicity's chocolates.

"I can't believe that she's cheating!" exclaimed Daisy.

"I knew she wouldn't be able to do it," said Holly gloating. "Not everyone has as much will power and determination as me."

Polly was disappointed in Felicity. "The best thing we can do to help Felicity is to hide these chocolates somewhere else. Then the next time she has a craving, there won't be any chocolate around," said Polly, quickly closing the lid and popping the box into her bag.

The fairies quietly made their way out of the back door and headed home.

\* \* \*

After school the next day, Felicity declined the invitation to Sparkles for a milkshake and instead headed straight home and straight into her 'sweetie' drawer for a desperately needed square of chocolate. She had been looking forward to this moment all day. Suddenly her heart stopped – where was her Secrets Box!? She was sure she had put it back into the drawer yesterday but it was gone!

Room by room she searched every cupboard, opened every drawer and looked under every piece of furniture until she was sure that the Secrets Box was definitely not in the house.

"What am I going to do?" squealed Felicity out loud, beside herself with worry. Not only did Felicity keep her secret supply of chocolate in the box, but she also kept all of her own secrets there too! She wrote every secret she had, in her best fairy handwriting, on a tiny piece of paper and stored it in her box.

The thought of someone reading her secrets was too much to bear and that night she couldn't sleep a wink.

"Where is my Secrets Box?" she murmured as she tossed and turned. "What if someone finds the box and opens it?!" she said out loud as she sat bolt upright in bed. "All those important secrets won't be secret any more. And what if they can't keep a secret and tell someone else!" It was no good. All the time the Secrets Box was missing Felicity wouldn't be able to rest.

\* \* \*

By the time Polly arrived at Felicity's house the next day to walk with her to school, Felicity was beside herself with worry!

"What in the fairy world have you been doing?" said Polly, climbing over the contents of Felicity's kitchen that were sprawled out all over her garden. Felicity emerged from a pile of kitchen utensils looking frantic and sleepy-eyed.

"I've lost something secret that I have to find and I can't stop until I do!" said Felicity, desperately searching through a drawer that she had already checked at least ten times!

"Can I help?" ventured Polly, feeling a little bad that she knew what Felicity was looking for and where it was.

"No, no. What I've lost is a secret. In fact it's lots of secrets and I'm the only one who can find it."

Polly got up. "Are you sure what

you've lost is such a big secret that it can't be shared?" asked Polly, trying to help Felicity admit that she had been eating chocolate.

"Oh it is way too big to share," said Felicity, carrying on with her search.

"I had better leave you to it then," said Polly flying off. "Don't be late for school."

* * *

At break-time, Polly called an emergency meeting under the Large Oak tree in the playing field.

"I'm afraid we've overdone it," she said seriously to Holly and Daisy. "Felicity just can't cope without chocolate. I went to her house and everything was everywhere!"

"What do you mean?" said Daisy, concerned.

"Felicity has turned her house inside out looking for her chocolate. I really thought we were doing the best thing by secretly hiding them from her but now I'm not so sure," said Polly, opening her bag and pulling out the Secrets Box.

"Oh no!" exclaimed Daisy. "She must be having a really tough time."

"But it's only been two weeks," complained Holly. "And I've been doing so well."

"Honestly," implored Polly, "if you could see Felicity, you'd come to the same conclusion as me. We'll have to give her the box back."

* * *

When the fairy friends reached Felicity's house after school, Felicity was nowhere to be seen.

They searched everywhere until Daisy finally found her asleep under the kitchen sink!

Quietly they climbed over the mess and gently woke her.

"Felicity, wake up. We've got your

box!" said Daisy, gently rocking
Felicity awake.

Sleepily, Felicity opened her eyes
and nearly cried when she saw her
Secrets Box.

"Where did you find it?" she asked,
sitting up and rubbing her eyes. "How
did you know this was what I was
looking for?" she added, confused.

"We took it, and we're sorry. We thought it was for the best," said Polly.

"Your secrets are safe with us," said Holly.

Felicity looked uneasy. It wasn't perfect that her friends knew all her secrets but at least she knew she could trust Holly, Polly and Daisy not to tell anyone else.

"That's very good of you," said Felicity. "Secrets like these are hard to keep safe. Do you absolutely promise never ever to tell another fairy?"

"Of course we do," said Polly reassuringly.

"Yes, definitely," said Daisy.

"Well, if it means that much to you that no one knows you cheated in our no-chocolate-eating pact then that's fine with me," said Holly. "But personally I think you're being a bit over the top."

"But what about the secret of me loving my stripy tights so much that I sometimes wear them in bed?" asked Felicity anxiously.

Holly, Polly and Daisy looked at each other in confusion.

"And the one about the library book – 'How to be a Best Friend' – that I borrowed months ago but haven't yet returned? And what about my fairy cake recipe? You promise you won't tell anyone my secret ingredient of fairy five-spice to give it an extra kick?" Felicity waffled non-stop.

Eventually Felicity finished reeling off her top secrets, only to find that her friends were rolling around on the floor in fits of laughter.

"Oh Felicity, no wonder your cakes taste so odd!" said Polly, hugging her friend.

Felicity Wishes looked blankly at

her friends and then slowly opened the lid of her Secrets Box. Her secrets were still nestled deep at the bottom of the box.

"You didn't read them?!" she said, suddenly realising her mistake.

"Of course we didn't!" chorused her friends. "They were your secrets."

"Well in that case it looks as though our pact is off!" said Holly, remembering the rules they made at the beginning. "I think we already know that your deepest darkest secret is that you're a chocoholic!"

Secrets you're
afraid to reveal

show unexpected surprises
when they're shared

# Truth Test

Felicity Wishes was fretting.
Tomorrow was the day of the Annual
Wish Test at the School of Nine
Wishes and she was sure she was
going to fail miserably.

"I'm just not very good at making
wishes," said Felicity, twiddling the
end of her wand.

"That's not true," said Daisy. "You
just need a little more practice."

"But I'm not what you'd call a
'natural', am I?" said Felicity glumly.

"None of us are," said Polly, trying to make Felicity feel better. "Just because we're fairies doesn't automatically mean we can make wishes."

"Arabella and Amy can, though," said Holly, pointing in the direction of two almost identical fairies practising their wand strokes on the other side of the playing field.

Arabella and Amy looked so similar that most fairies thought they were twins.

In fact they were not just best friends but best friends who did everything together: they shopped together for the same clothes, copied each other's hairstyles, and even had the same handwriting!

The most amazing thing about them though was that they were both

naturals at making wishes.

Even in their first wish class, on their first day at the School of Nine Wishes, Miss Powers, the wish teacher, was astounded by their advanced capabilities.

"I might ask them for some top tips," said Felicity, watching in awe as perfectly shaped wish stars flew from their wands in a synchronised pattern.

"You'll be lucky," giggled Holly. "Arabella and Amy never let anyone know the secret of their success."

Felicity sighed. Maybe she would never be good at making wishes.

✳ ✳ ✳

By the time the school day was over, Felicity's nerves had got the better of her. Everywhere she looked, fairies were swishing their wands with amazing effects, practising for tomorrow's competition. But Felicity still couldn't even make a basic wish without it going wrong! She had no other choice but to ask for Arabella and Amy's help.

"Hello," said Felicity, calling out into the empty classroom. "Is anyone here?"

Arabella and Amy always stayed behind after school in chemistry class, mixing new and more refined grades of sparkledust. One day, they hoped to win the Fairy Scientists of the Year Award.

"Oh!" squealed Amy, nearly spilling the sparkling pot in her hand. "You startled me. It's Felicity Wishes, isn't it?"

"Yes," said Felicity. "You'd think with a name like this that I'd be good at making wishes, but unfortunately I'm not."

"Well, it's the Annual Wish Test tomorrow so you'd better get practising!" joked Amy as she carefully poured some sparkledust into a large bubbling beaker.

"Well, actually, that's why I'm here," said Felicity sheepishly. "Where's Arabella?"

"She's gone home to rest her arm for tomorrow. She twisted it making a double-loop rainbow shower wish this afternoon."

Felicity sighed. She knew it was unlikely that she would ever be able to make a basic wish, let alone a double-loop rainbow shower wish!

"I was wondering if you could give me some top tips on wish-making?" asked Felicity hopefully.

Amy stopped for a moment and put down the beaker. "How bad exactly are you?" she asked curiously.

Felicity got out her wand, put down her bag and showed Amy her best standard swing.

"Hmm," said Amy, raising her eyebrows and desperately trying to think of a kind way to be honest. "I think there's room for improvement but, I'm afraid, you've left it a bit too late to practise."

"Oh, not to worry," said Felicity, trying not to sound too disappointed.

"I'll just have to do my best on the day. Thanks, anyway." Slowly Felicity picked up her bag and turned to go.

"Wait!" called Amy before she got to the door. "Can you keep a secret?"

Felicity turned round immediately. She loved secrets. "Yes," she answered truthfully.

"Then give me five minutes while I pack up and I'll take you somewhere that will have your standard swing gaining you top marks in minutes!"

* * *

Amy and Felicity flew out of the School of Nine Wishes, over the school playing fields and along a long and winding path until they reached Nine Wish Wood.

Deep in the middle of the wood was the only place in Little Blossoming where silver-star flowers grew. The pollen was the essential ingredient in all grades of sparkledust as it contained special magical properties.

By the time Felicity and Amy arrived at the wood, darkness had fallen and the only sound to be heard was the rustling trees.

"Where are you?" whispered Felicity, reaching out into the dark.

"I'm over here," said Amy giggling, turning on a small torch.

The torchlight threw strange shadows all around them.

"How is this going to improve my standard swing?" asked Felicity, feeling a little uneasy in the dark.

"Follow me and I'll show you," said Amy as she tiptoed towards the base of a large birch tree.

Felicity followed Amy over to the tree. "What are we looking for?" asked Felicity, hearing her tummy rumble and wishing she'd gone straight home for tea instead.

"Shhhh!" said Amy, putting her finger to her lips and shining the torch on her watch. "Any minute now!"

Suddenly the silver-star flowers burst open to reveal beautiful petals that glistened with magic dust. Felicity was speechless – she had never seen anything as beautiful before.

Quickly Amy took hold of Felicity's

wand and gently tapped it in the
centre of one of the flowers,
and then she did the
same with her
own wand.

Just as quickly as the petals opened,
they suddenly closed.

"Wow!" said Felicity, inspecting the
glow that now surrounded her wand.
There was no need for Amy's torch
any more.

"Stunning, isn't it?" said Amy. "Go on!" she said excitedly, "try your standard swing now!"

Felicity stood nervously, corrected the position of her feet, pushed her shoulders back, closed her eyes, focused on her wish, and swung with all her might.

"WOW!" said Felicity even louder than before. "It was like the wand swung itself!"

"And it was a hundred-per-cent perfect!" said Amy. "Even a professional couldn't have done better."

* * *

On the way back, Amy explained to Felicity that she hadn't always used the silver-star flower to help her wish-making. Several years ago, Arabella and herself entered an international competition and the pressure was on for them to perform. Arabella, as always, performed her wish without a

hitch but nerves had consumed Amy
and, before she knew it, she had
dropped her wand at the most crucial
part of the test.

Amy's failure to gain even standard marks made her feel as if she'd let down her best friend, the school, Miss Powers, and in fact the whole of Little Blossoming!

"It was awful," said Amy. "I vowed never to make wishes competitively again, and no matter how much Arabella and Miss Powers tried to help I never got my confidence back... until the day I wandered into the wood and discovered the silver-star flowers."

Felicity looked shocked. "You mean you use the magic dust in competitions now?"

"Every time!" said Amy. "But you mustn't tell anyone; even Arabella doesn't know. She thought my confidence and ability came back with her help, not with the magic dust."

Felicity looked down at her glowing wand. "How long does the dust last for?" she asked.

"Just twelve hours," said Amy. "If you want to use it for the test then you'll have to top it up tomorrow." And with that Amy flew off into the night, leaving Felicity still staring at her golden wand.

\* \* \*

All that night Felicity lay awake worrying, and for the first time that week it wasn't about her own wish test. She was worried that Amy's confidence depended on the silver-star magic dust. Amy was once a naturally good wish-maker and Felicity felt certain that she could be one again if only she could believe in herself.

\* \* \*

The next day at school, Felicity met Holly, Polly and Daisy under the Large Oak tree.

"Ready for the test?" asked Polly. "Did Amy give you any top tips?"

"No, and yes," said Felicity awkwardly.

"Well?" said Daisy, excitedly. "Have you discovered the secret of the most talented wish-maker in the school?"

Felicity thought carefully for a moment.

"Confidence," she said. "It's the most magical ingredient there is!"

"That's easy for her to say," said Holly. "Confidence comes with success which, I have to say, is pretty limited with us four!"

"Not necessarily," said Felicity thoughtfully. "If we all encourage and believe in each other, success may just follow."

Felicity's own words repeated in her head and she suddenly had a great brainwave! "I've got to go!" she said looking up at the clock. "I'll see you at the test later on."

✳ ✳ ✳

Felicity flew as fast as her wings would take her. She knew she could never betray Amy's trust by telling Fairy Godmother, Miss Powers, or even Arabella her secret. But she could do something else, and if it worked then Amy would no longer have to keep her secret safe.

"Pass me your wand," whispered Felicity to Amy as she stood in the lunch-time queue. "I'm just off to you-know-where and I can do yours at the same time, if you like?"

"Thanks, Felicity," said Amy grinning. "I was hoping to get out of my next class early to fly there myself. Make sure you get a good coating – I really want this test to go well!"

Felicity winked and waved at Amy. "See you later!" she said and disappeared in a flutter of two wings.

"Who was that?" asked Arabella who was queuing in front of Amy.

"Oh, that, erm, was, erm, Felicity Wishes," said Amy stumbling over her words. "She's terrible at making wishes so I've, erm, been giving her a few, erm, last minute tips for the competition."

"Well, you are the best wish-maker in the school," said Arabella cheerfully.

Amy felt awful. She didn't like telling fibs to her best friend but she also didn't want to let her down.

\* \* \*

Finally, the Annual Wish Test had begun. Every single fairy in the School of Nine Wishes stood in their relevant groups waiting nervously for their name to be called.

One by one, they stood on the stage in front of Fairy Godmother and Miss Powers and performed the best wish they could. The fairies gave it everything they had.

The mark they received would not only determine what class they would be in next year, but it would also go towards deciding what type of fairy they would be when they left school. Most of the fairies already knew what they wanted to be so tried as hard as they could to impress their teachers.

"Felicity Wishes," called Fairy Godmother, reading from her list.

"Good luck!" called Holly, Polly and Daisy as Felicity walked up on to the stage.

With quivering wings, Felicity tried to focus her mind and forget about Amy for the moment. She took a deep breath and then gently swept her wand high above her head, concentrating hard on her wish.

Felicity's wish was as perfect as it had been the night before in Nine Wish Wood.

"Wonderful!" said Fairy Godmother, clapping enthusiastically. "Felicity, you should be very proud of yourself. You'll definitely go up a class!"

Felicity beamed and skipped off the stage to join her friends.

"That was great!" chorused Polly and Daisy.

"You must have done quite a lot of last minute practice," said Holly. "You've gone from being truly awful to truly magnificent!"

Felicity anxiously turned to find Amy. She was pleased that she did well in the test but was more concerned how Amy had done. Felicity's heart sank when she saw a tearful Amy hugging Arabella. She was sure her plan would have worked but maybe she was wrong.

"I'm sorry," said Felicity.

"Sorry for what?" asked Arabella. "You've no need to be sorry for Amy –

she was the star of the show!"

"But I thought you were upset?" said Felicity confused.

"No, I'm just so shocked and pleased at the praise from Fairy Godmother. She's put me up two classes."

"Amy was marvellous," said Arabella proudly. "In fact I've never seen her perform a wish that well before. I think I may have a bit of catching up to do!" she added with a giggle.

Amy leaned forward and whispered in Felicity's ear. "Thanks for collecting the magic dust. You did a good job – it's never felt so powerful!"

71

"Your talent today is purely down to you, not the magic dust!" whispered Felicity back.

Amy frowned with confusion.

"I've got a secret to share with you too," continued Felicity forgetting to whisper. "I never went to Nine Wish Wood at lunch-time!"

"You never went to Nine Wish Wood?" said Arabella, catching the end of the conversation. "What sort of secret is that?"

"One that shows belief, encouragement, confidence and success!" said Felicity giving Amy a huge squeeze!

The biggest secret that makes your dreams come true

is believing in yourself

If you enjoyed this book, why not try another of these fantastic story collections?

Clutter Clean-out

Designer Drama

Newspaper Nerves

Star Surprise

Enchanted Escape

Friends Forever

Sensational Secrets

Whispering Wishes

# Also available in the Felicity Wishes range:

## Felicity Wishes: Mix-ups and Magic

Felicity makes a wish for each of her unhappy friends,
but her wishes are a little mixed-up...

## Felicity Wishes: Snowflakes and Sparkledust

It is time for spring to arrive in Little Blossoming but there is a problem and
winter is staying put. Can Felicity Wishes get the seasons back on track?

## Felicity Wishes: Secrets and Surprises

Felicity Wishes is planning her birthday party but it seems none of her friends can come. Will Felicity end up celebrating her birthday alone?

## Felicity Wishes: Friendship and Fairyschool

It is nearly time for Felicity Wishes to leave fairy school. But poor Felicity has no idea what kind of fairy she wants to be!

Felicity Wishes has lots to say in these fantastic little books:

### Little Book of Love

### Little Book of Peace

### Little Book of Hiccups

### Little Book of Every Day Wishes

### Little Book of Fun